AF406590

J.C. HULSEY BOOKS

DOKE WALKER
A WESTERN SHORT

J.C. HULSEY

For information contact: info@jchulseybooks.com
Cover Art by Michael Thomas
Cover Design by J.C. Hulsey Books
Published by J.C. Hulsey Books
September 2020
10 9 8 7 6 5 4 3 2 1

CHAPTER ONE

"You gonna fix that busted fence today?" Wyatt Snow, my foreman spoke.

"I might," I said, rather hateful. "Right after I run into town and take care of a little business."

"What kind of business you got in town?"

"If you must know, it's personal and don't concern you, so just butt out and take care of your own business."

"I reckon I can do that," he says.

"You know you can't keep shirking your chores like this? I'm getting too blamed old to do mine and yours. Can't that trip to town wait 'til you get the fence mended?"

"I guess since you put it that way, I'll take care of it now."

I hooked up the wagon and loaded all the posts, wire and the rest of the stuff I needed.

"I'm gonna grab a bite to eat before I head out."

"Okay, but you're burning daylight."

"I know what time it is," I snapped at him.

I drained the last of the pot into my cup and finished it off, wiping my mouth with the back of my hand.

"Well, I reckon I better get started. See you around sundown." I jumped up in the wagon, hollered to the team and the wagon started moving.

"Hold on! You forgot this." He tossed a canteen to me. I caught it and waved to him as we pulled around the corner of the house. I wasn't hardly out of sight and my shirt was already soaked with sweat. I removed my hat and wiped my forehead with my sleeve. I sure wasn't looking forward to this job. Sometimes I think having a job in town would be better than this. But then I'd think about being cooped up inside all day and think this is probably better for somebody like me. Being stuck inside all the time would be too much like jail for me.

It took three long days to repair that busted fence. I wish we still had enough hands to do this kind of stuff, but we don't. Ever since Pa died things have gone downhill. Amos and Angus Cantrell and of course Wyatt Snow, the Foreman, were the only ones to stick with us. The twins were out tending the cattle which was quite a chore. I couldn't ask them to do something I could do myself, so here I am twisting wire and repairing the fence. Each day a little after sundown, I headed to the house where I gobbled down whatever Wyatt set in front of me and went straight to bed. Didn't even take my clothes off. Wyatt woke me early each morning, before sunup.

When I twisted that last piece of wire, I leaned on the post and looked back at the patched fence. I felt a little proud of the job I had done. I figured Pa would be proud too. He always had a hard time getting me to do anything. But Pa's gone now and I got to buck up and act like an owner of this broken-down ranch.

It was supper time when I rolled into the yard. Amos was just coming out of the house.

"Howdy, Doke," he said. "You get that fence patched?"

"Yes, I did, and am I glad it's done," I replied. "How's the cows doing? Got plenty of grass?"

"We had to move them over to the next pasture. The grass done wore plumb to the ground. Gonna take a heap of rain to git it to come back. Reckon I better git back out there so's Angus can come in and eat. See you later." He waved as he climbed in the saddle, spurred his horse and left the yard at a gallop.

I went in the house and Wyatt asked, "Git her all fixed up?"

"Yeah, and I don't need nobody to go and check to see if I done it right. I done a good job."

"Wasn't gonna say nothing," he shot back. "You gonna wash up and eat afore you head into town?"

"I figured I'd eat at the café in town and maybe git a bath at the barber shop," I said. "If you don't mind, that is."

"Would it make any difference if I did mind? I reckon you're a growed man and you're gonna do what you want no matter what anybody says."

"I'm leaving as soon as I saddle my horse. Be gone a couple days, maybe more. You can handle everything without me, can't you?"

"Why don't you wait 'til morning, take the wagon and pick up supplies while you're there?" he said. "Should be something at the Feed Store."

"What's at the Feed Store?" I asked.

"Can't remember, but there's always somethin'"

"Okay, I reckon I can wait 'til morning. You got any grub and coffee?"

"Set yourself down and I'll git you something."

"You need anything from town?" I asked

"I can't think of nothing, but I do wish you wouldn't wear your guns to town," he said mournfully. "Them guns could git you killt one of these days."

"Like you said, I'm a grown man and a man, don't go no place without his guns, besides you know I'm very good with'em."

"Yeah, I know how much time you spent practicing and I also know you think you're good, but remember this, there's always somebody a little bit better, a little bit faster and I need you to come home alive preferably."

"I'll be careful." With that, I turned and went into my room, splashed a little water on my face, undressed and passed out on the bed.

Wyatt didn't wake me the next morning, so it was late when I woke. "How come you didn't wake me?" I fussed at him.

"I figured a growing boy needs his rest. Set down and eat somethin' afore you go. By the way, that's the last of the bacon."

I finished off the eggs and bacon with about four cups of Wyatt's coffee and rushed out the front door, climbed in the wagon, where I had left it sit overnight, slapped the reins against the rump of the horse and headed for town.

CHAPTER TWO

The ride to town wasn't very exciting, but I held the reins lightly and let the horses make their own speed. I leaned against the back of the seat and cast my eyes toward the heavens. I was always amazed at God's creation whenever I took the time to gaze at the clouds and the way they seemed to change shape as I looked at them. They almost blocked out the sun, which made me wish for this cloud cover when I was repairing the fence. It was sure a peaceful feeling and I wished I could bottle it and keep it with me forever, but that's just dreaming, cause the bottom line is life is more than a few daydreams. It seems something always comes along and spoils it.

I straightened up as we reached the outskirts of town. The sign read, *You're now entering Crockett Texas. Pop. 507.* I drove to the livery stable where old man Garret was standing in the doorway whittling on a chunk of wood. He looked up, saw me, folded his knife, put it in his shirt pocket, "Howdy Doke, I thought you'd be in town 'afore this."

"Had a little chore to do first, but I'm here now. Anything happening, I should know about?" I asked him.

"They's a hard-case come into town yesterday. Done killed that young kid, Lenny Burkhalter. You know the one always acting like he was a fast gun. If'n I's you, I wouldn't go in the saloon."

"That's just it, Mr. Garret, you ain't me," I told him as he looked at the floor. "What'd the sheriff do about it?"

"You know Sheriff Blasingame. He done what he always does," he said, shaking his head. "Nothing. Said it was self-defense."

"You reckon somebody ortta have a talk with this man?" I asked.

"Yeah, I reckon, but I don't reckon it ortta be you," he said. "Why you wanna git involved?"

"Like I said, somebody needs to talk to him," I told him, turned and started toward the saloon. I stopped and said, "Take care of my wagon, will you?"

"Sure thing, but I still say you ortta stay outa it."

The saloon was extremely quiet for this time of day. Didn't even hear any piano music. I stepped up on the boardwalk and stopped to peer over the doors. A dark hombre with dusty black clothes and a. 45 slung low on his him was leaning against the bar with a glass in his hand facing the crowd, if you could call it a crowd. Only two people in there with this yahoo.

I pushed through the doors and stopped just inside.

"Well, lookee here," the man said. "We got us a real fancy gunman come to see us. You are here to see us ain't you, Kid?"

"That depends," I said calmly, releasing the leather tie down from the hammer of my pistol.

"You better think over what you're doing," the man said a little loudly.

"I thought it over and all I see is a low life that gunned down a young kid without giving him a chance."

"You mean that snot-nosed kid that threw down on me when I come into town? That who you're talking about? Sheriff done called it self-defense."

"Our sheriff don't always see the big picture."

The man had an icy tone to his voice that sent cold chills down my spine, but I had gone too far to back down now, so I straightened up and said as calmly as I could, "I reckon it's your move, stranger."

He was fast, really fast, but I was a tad faster. He had barely cleared leather when the slug from my forty-five entered just to the right of his heart. He looked down as the crimson stain spread across his shirt. Then he looked up at me and mouthed the words. "You can't kill me, you're just a kid," then he slumped forward onto the sawdust floor right after his gun slipped from his hand. The blood quickly made a puddle that the sawdust soaked up.

The saloon doors burst open and the Sheriff Blasingame rushed in with his gun in his hand. He stopped when he saw the dead body, then turned to face me. "You do this, Walker?" he asked, holding his gun toward me.

"I reckon I did. It seems the law in this town wanted to let this scum stay in town and threaten the folks." "Maybe you better come to the office with me and let's have a little talk," he waved his gun indicating I should follow him.

I removed the spent cartridge from the cylinder and replaced it with a new one, then slid my gun into the holster.

I looked at the sheriff still holding his weapon in my direction. "I'm more than willing to go with you on one condition," I told him.

"What condition?" he asked.

"Holster your hog leg and I'll follow you to the jail."

He did as I asked, shaking his head as if he didn't realize he was holding a gun. He took off out the door of the saloon and I followed.

CHAPTER THREE

We reached the jail and he opened the door and motioned for me to go ahead of him. I did, stopping just inside the door and stepping to the side as he entered. He walked to his desk, sat down and removed his hat, placing it on the table top.

"How come you did that?" he asked, looking into my eyes. "I would have run him outta town if there had been any more trouble."

"Sheriff, I understand this is a tough job, but sometimes somebody like me needs to help. I understand he killed Lenny Burkhalter. You know yourself that Lenny wasn't no match for somebody like him."

"I want you to listen to me and listen real close. I'm the law here in Crockett and I'll say who stays or goes in this town and you better keep those guns of yours in the holsters or I might have to lock you up. Now get outta here."

I was leaving the jail when I noticed three men ride up and stop in front of the saloon. It seems the town was attracting the scum today. They were very noisy as they went inside. I started across the street when I saw him.

He was a giant of a man with long curly red hair and beard. He was dressed in dirty buckskins wearing thigh high moccasins and was carrying an old flintlock cap and ball rifle. One look into his steel gray eyes told me he was in town on business. What kind of business? I was pretty sure I knew. I had heard recently that a squaw married to a white man had been murdered. It hadn't been a quick death. It was long and dragged out, no doubt inflicting much pain, before she passed from this world. I had also heard that the three men who did it were going around bragging, how that squaw squealed and hollered, before she died. I found that hard to believe. I had seen more'n my share of Indians die, both men and women. Not a one of them squealed or hollered. Instead, they died spitting in the face of their killer.

I walked up to the red giant and introduced myself. "I'm Doke Walker. I'd guess you're looking for three men?"

He nodded without telling his name.

"There's three of them. That old flintlock of yours ain't gonna be much good after the first shot. You'll surely die trying. If I was you, and I'm not, but I would accept any help that was offered."

He spoke for the first time. "You offering?"

"I reckon I am. Those men are in the saloon right across the street. Anytime you're ready, I am too."

He nodded and stepped into the street heading for the saloon with purpose in his steps. I had to hustle to match his giant steps. We reached the front of the saloon.

As he started to step up on the boardwalk, I said, "Hold on a minute, we need some kind of plan before we go in there. What'd you say I take the one on your left? You take the one on the right. That'll leave the one in the middle. If I'm still standing, I'll take him too."

He cocked the flintlock, poured a little powder in the pocket and went through the door with me right behind him. He moved to the right of the door and I slid to the left.

The room got deathly quiet. The men we were looking for slammed down their glasses and turned.

"Well, well, lookee here, Virgil," the greasy haired man spoke through broken rotten teeth. "It looks like a mountain man. I hear they favor squaw meat. Is that right squaw man? You partial to squaw meat?"

"Take it easy," I said quietly. "He's trying to rattle you. When I give the word, you lift that rifle and fire." I spoke to the men "You boys caught up on your praying?"

"We don't pray," a second weasel faced man said quickly. "Why you asking that?"

"'Cause the three of you are going to meet your maker today."

They reached for their weapons and just as quickly the three men were lying in the sawdust as the crimson colored liquid began to puddle under and around them. I looked at my new friend and he looked at me while he reloaded his rifle. I rejected the spent cartridges and replaced them.

I had just slid my pistol in the holster when the saloon doors were flung open and the sheriff rushed into the room with his .45 in his hand.

"Alright," he said with authority, "What's going on here? Walker, you involved in this? I thought you heard me when I told you . . ."

"I heard you, Sheriff, but this here is a special case."

"I don't care about no special case, I told you I would lock you up and that's what I'm gonna do." He pointed his weapon toward me and my new friend.

I looked at the giant, expecting him to speak up, but he remained stone faced silent.

"It was self-defense, Sheriff," I told him. "You can ask anybody."

"I don't need to ask nobody nothing," he said, looking around the room. "In fact, why don't the two of you lay your weapons on the bar and let's take a walk over to the jail."

The giant cocked his rifle, which caused the sheriff to swing his pistol to cover the man.

"Hold on, partner," I said, laying my hand on his arm. "Let's not make this any worse than it is. The sheriff is only doing his job. Ain't that right, Sheriff?"

I could see his hand shaking as he said, "That's right. Just doing my job. Now you fellows come on peaceable like."

The giant un-cocked his rifle, but didn't place it on the bar, instead he settled it across his arms.

"Come on," I told him. "Let's go with this lawman. We'll be outta there in no time at all."

CHAPTER FOUR

The sheriff holstered his gun and turned, expecting us to follow.

"Man ain't got a lotta sense, turning his back on us like that," growled the giant.

"Come on," I said, and started following behind the sheriff.

We entered the jail right behind the sheriff. He walked over and sat down at his desk, then turned around facing us. I noticed his eye twitched as he spoke. "You gentlemen want to tell me how come there's three dead bodies in the saloon?"

Again, I looked at my friend, expecting him to answer.

"I think I can explain, Sheriff," I spoke up. "Those three men killed this man's wife. They've been bragging about it for a couple weeks now. This man came to town looking for them and he found them. If you'll bother talking to the witnesses that saw what happened, you'll find it was self-defense. It's a simple matter, if you'll look into it."

"If it was this man's wife, as you said, what's your interest in all this, especially after our little talk?"

"I could see he was outnumbered. I always figured a fight should be fair, so I stepped in."

"What's your name, Stranger," he looked at the giant.

The man didn't say anything. Just stood there like a wooden Indian.

I reached over and touched his arm. "Do you know your name?"

He turned those steel gray eyes toward me as a silver tear slid down his cheek and shook his head.

"Sheriff, I don't think he remembers his name. He's been in the mountains a long time."

"Surely he's got a name. What am I gonna put in the paperwork?"

"Why don't you put Red Walker?"

"Ain't that your name, Walker?"

"Yeah, that's my name and I would be mighty proud to share it with my new friend. Is that okay with you, Red?" looking up into his eyes.

He straightened up to his full height, sniffed and smiled with the whitest teeth I've ever seen.

He looked at the sheriff and proclaimed, "my name is Red Walker."

"Alright, Mr. Walker," the sheriff said, the two Walkers, I reckon you can go, but would you do something for me, Walker?"

"Sure, Sheriff, "I said. "What can we do for you?"

"Please don't shoot nobody else, at least not in my town."

"We'll do our best to stay outta trouble." I tipped my hat, turned, touched Red on the arm and we left together.

We had just stepped off the sidewalk when I saw her coming out of the general store. "Hold on a minute, Red. I need to do something, but I don't want to leave you. I want to talk to you about going back to the ranch with me, but right now I need to go see someone. Will you stay in town until we talk?"

He nodded his head and sat down on the sidewalk.

CHAPTER FIVE

I rushed across the street and caught up with her just as she stepped off the sidewalk.

"Where you going?" I asked her. "Why don't you come up and sit with me on the swing? I'd like to talk to you."

"I've got someplace I need to be," she said, "but if you're still here when I come back, I'd be proud to sit with you."

"Is this place you got to be very far?"

"Not far, but I've got to hurry. I'm running late as it is," she said, turning away, "Like I said, if you're here when I come back, I'll sit with you."

"How about I go with you?"

"No. I don't think you should. This is something personal I have to do and really I don't think you would enjoy yourself."

"I just want to be with you. What's wrong with that?"
"Nothing, I reckon, but this is personal, like I said. It doesn't concern you."

"Let me be the judge of that?"

"Okay, but I don't think you should."

I took her arm and said, "Alright, lead the way."

She looked up at me and shook her head, pulled her arm loose, then took off at a brisk pace.

"Wait a minute, what's the hurry?"

"I told you I was late, so if you're coming, keep up."

She hurried down the street and turned into the alley beside the Feed Store. She slowed when she reached the back of the building. She craned her neck and looked around the corner.

"What'cha looking for?" I asked.

"Nothing really, just looking," as she stepped around the corner and headed for the back door of the Feed Store. She stepped up on the small porch and reached for the door knob. It was locked.

She stepped off the porch and looked around, then spotted a window about half way up the back wall.

"Lift me up to that window so's I can look inside?"

"Will you tell me what's going on?"

"Please," she begged with her voice and her slate blue eyes.

"Alright, put your foot in my hands and I'll lift you up as high as I can." She placed her tiny foot in my hands and I lifted.

"A little higher," she said.

I strained and lifted a little more.

"What do you see?" as I held her up by the small window?

"I can't see anything, it's too dark," she said. "Hold on a minute. There's something in front of the door. It could be a body. Let me down and let's try the door again."

I let her down and she rushed to the door, twisting and pulling on the knob.

"We done tried that and ain't nothing changed since then." I exclaimed. "What'd you mean a body? You gonna tell me what's going on?" I asked her as she tried the doorknob again."

"Oh, alright," she shrugged her shoulders. "I reckon since you're here, you're gonna know sooner or later. Mr. Flannery is a killer," she said emphatically.

"Why would you say something like that?" I asked, surprised at her accusation. "Why would you say that?"

"I heard him and Mr. Ferguson auguring and Mr. Flannery shouted he was gonna kill him," she said with a certainty in her voice.

"Lots of folks say things they don't mean."

"But Mr. Ferguson didn't show up for work this morning over at the freight office." There were tears in her eyes as she spoke.

"Okay. Okay, don't cry on me," I said. "Why don't you go inside the store and into the back room?"

"And what would I tell Mr. Flannery about going in his back room?"

"I guess you're right. He would be suspicious, especially if he killed him."

She twisted the doorknob again.

"It's still locked."

"I've got to do something," she whined. "He's a murderer. I got no doubt about that. Wait a cotton-picking minute. I know how we can check the back room."

"How?" I asked.

"You go in and start talking to Mr. Flannery and I'll slip by and go into the back," she was excited.

"What am I supposed to talk about?"

"Well, you are the owner of a ranch. Talk to him about feed for your cattle. Oh, you'll think of something. Come on, let's go." She grabbed my hand and started pulling me toward the front of the building.

We reached the door and she got as close to the wall as she could.

"Go on in and start talking. Try to get his back to the door and I'll slip by. He'll never see me." She gave me a little shove. "

"Okay, but you be careful, will you?"

"Of course, careful is my middle name," she said. "Now go ahead."

I went inside and walked right up to stand beside Mr. Flannery where he was bent over behind the counter.

He stood and gave a little squeak. "Don't you know better than to slip up on a body? Almost gave me a heart attack. What can I do for you, Walker, ain't it? Frank Walker's boy?"

"Yes sir, that's who I am, Doke Walker."

"Sorry about your pa. He was a good man. Always paid his bills right on time. Understand you're the one I'll be dealing with from now on."

"Yes sir, that's right and right now I'd like to look at some feed. I heard you have a special mixture that's supposed to help the cattle gain weight."

"Sure do, it's right over here," he turned to face the front of the building just as Imogene started in the door. I reached and grabbed his arm, maybe a little too hard, because he turned putting his back to her.

"What did you do that for," he asked rubbing his arm.

"I'm sorry, sometimes I don't know my own strength. Did I hurt you?"

"No harm done, I reckon. How come you grabbed me? I thought you wanted to see that special mixture?"

"I do, but first I wanted you to check and see if there's a special order for the ranch. Snow said something about it when I left."

"No ain't nothing on order. He say what it was?"

"No, he probably got it mixed up. He's been doing that a lot lately."

I watched as Imogene slipped past and into the back room. I took a deep breath and said, "I reckon we can look at that special mix now."

We walked across the room and he said, "This is it, I'm mighty proud of it. It's gonna make things a whole lot easier for fattening up the cattle."

"How much is it gonna cost?" I asked, looking at the door to the back room.

"Well, since you're the new owner of the Walker spread and you'll be the first one to buy a batch of this special mix, I'm gonna give you a really good deal." He was smiling from ear to ear.

"Maybe I better talk it over with Snow. After all, he's really the one in charge of that kind of stuff," I said, turning and heading for the front door.

"But . . . but I thought you was the owner?" he stammered.

"I am, but I'm still learning. Thanks for showing that mix to me. I'll let you know what we decide." I hurried out the door, turned and ran down the alley.

Imogene was sitting on the little porch with her head in her hands. Her face was as white as a ghost.

"You okay," I asked, sitting beside her and touching her shoulder.

She turned and threw her arms around me. "He's in there, and he's dead."

"You saw him?" I asked, enjoying her arms around me.

"Yes, his body was blocking the door. That's why we couldn't get it open. I pulled it to the side and came out. I've. . . we've got to do something."

"We'll figure it out," I told her. "Have you told Sheriff Blasingame?"

"No, and I don't know if I want to or not," she said shaking her head. "Everybody knows what a lazy good for nothing he is."

"But he is the sheriff," I told her. "I don't think it would hurt to approach him and feel him out. Maybe this'll be the one time he does the right thing. Come on, I'll go with you."

CHAPTER SIX

I took her hand and we headed back through the alley and down the street to the sheriff's office.

He was half way out the door when he looked and saw us heading his direction. "What do you want now, Walker? You ain't shot no more folks, have you?"

"No, Sheriff, I ain't shot nobody since the last one. We, well I mean, me and Imogene here, got something you need to hear. Can we go back in your office?"

"I can't imagine what two kids would have to say that's so important, but come on, I'll listen." He stepped inside leaving the door ajar indicating we should come inside.

He stomped across the floor and settled in his chair behind the paper littered desk. He calmly lifted his boots and placed them on the corner of the desk, knocking some of the papers on the floor.

"Okay," he said, yawning to show us he really wasn't interested in anything we had to say. "I'm listening."

"Go ahead Imogene," I said. "Tell him."

She opened her mouth and then closed it, looking at me as if she wanted me to tell him, so I began, "We think there's been a murder, and we know who done it."

Sheriff Blasingame dropped one boot to the floor and asked, in his unconcerned voice, "who got murdered and who done it?"

"Mr. Flannery killed Mr. Ferguson," Imogene blurted out as if she couldn't keep it inside no more.

Now the sheriff dropped his other foot to the floor and started to stand, then sat back in the chair.

"You talking 'bout Flannery, the Feed Store owner?" he asked with surprise.

"Yes," said Imogene. "He killed him."

"He's supposed to have killed Ferguson, the clerk at the Freight Office? That what you're saying?"

"That's what we're saying," said Imogene excitedly.

"You're both loco. Them two men have been friends for years. Besides Flannery is one of the leading citizens of this town. He even ran for mayor last election."

"But I heard him threaten to kill him," Imogene said.

"Hold on, a cotton-picking minute. You saying what I think you're saying?" he looked at both of us with a questioning look on his face. "You didn't actually see anybody kill anybody. Is that what you're sayin'?"

"But, Sheriff, I did see the dead body." Imogene was whining again, "Ain't you even gonna look into it?"

"Did you see this dead body, Walker?" he asked looking directly at me.

"Well," I hesitated.

"I didn't think so. I ortta lock the two of you up and throw away the key. You should know better than to come in here and accuse one of the town's leading citizens of killing his friend. Now, git on outa here or I might just throw you in that cell back yonder. Go on. Git!"

"Come on, Imogene," I took her hand and started for the door.

"You don't need to be spreading them rumors around town neither, or I will lock you up. You hear me?"

"We hear you," I told him as we left the building.

"I told you he was good for nothing," said Imogene. "Now what're we gonna do?"

"We'll think of something, don't worry," I assured her.

She stopped quickly jerking her hand from mine, "I know who we can tell," she was grinning. "Mrs. Benifield."

"The mayor's wife?" I asked. "What makes you think she'll listen any more than the sheriff?"

"We have to convince her. If we can convince her, then she can convince the mayor and then we'll see justice at work."

She took my hand again and started pulling me to the east end of town where the wealthy folks lived.

The mayor's house was at the far end of the street and was one of the better houses on the street.

"You sure about this?" I asked her, stopping just outside the little gate. "We could just forget about it. It really ain't none of our concern, after all."

"When the law has been broken, it should be the concern of all law-abiding citizens to see that the wrong has been righted," she said, reaching down, sliding the little wire off the gate and pushing it open.

"Come on, Doke. Don't quit on me now," she looked at me with those slate blue eyes and right at that moment I would have walked across burning coals to please her.

I stepped through the gate and followed her to the front door. She lifted her hand to knock, then hesitated.

"Having second thoughts, are you?" I asked.

"No," she said and proceeded to knock.

"Just a minute," a woman's voice from inside said.

CHAPTER SEVEN

The door opened and a gray-haired lady in her late forties, dressed in a blue and white dress asked, "Why, hello there, Imogene, and you, you're Doke Walker, aren't you?"

"Yes ma'am, that's right." I said, removing my hat and twisting it in my hands.

"Well, don't stand there on the porch, come on in. I was just making a pitcher of lemonade. Would you care for a glass?" she turned back and asked with inquiring eyes.

"That sounds real nice, thank you Ma'am," I said.

"Have a seat there on the settee, I'll get some glasses and see if I can scare up some cookies too. Be right back." She hurried from the room.

"Are you gonna tell her or you gonna lay it off on me like you did with the sheriff?" I asked her.

"I'll tell her, I just have to find the right words," she said. "But you could maybe be a little more supportive."

"I'm here, ain't I? Cain't get more supportive than that, I don't reckon."

Mrs. Benifield came in carrying a tray with three glasses filled to the brim with this golden liquid and right beside the glasses were some sugar cookies, my favorite.

"Here you go," she said, handing Imogene a glass and then one to me. "Help yourself to the cookies, that is if you want some."

"Oh yeah," I said, grabbing a couple cookies and taking a bite. "Umm. These are great."

"I glad you like them. Now what did you want to tell me?" she looked first at me, then at Imogene. "It sounded very important."

"It is important," rushed Imogene, placing her glass back on the tray. "A man has been murdered and the sheriff won't even listen to us."

"I see," Mrs. Benifield said. "Who was murdered?"

"Mr. Flannery killed Mr. Ferguson," Imogene was whining. "I know he did."

"How do you know this?" asked Mrs. Benifield. "Did you see him do this horrible thing?"

"No ma'am, I didn't see him do it, but I know he did. I did see Mr. Ferguson's body in the back of the Feed Store."

"Alright calm down and tell me everything from the beginning."

"Well, I was on my way home from a late night of choir practice at the church, and I heard them in the alley by the Feed Store. I slowed down and hopped up on the sidewalk and pressed myself against the wall. They were both arguing about something. I never did hear what it was about, but then I heard just as plain as I'm hearing you right now. Mr. Flannery said in a slow even voice quieter than before, "I'm gonna kill you." I'd heard enough, so I slid along the wall in the opposite direction until I was away from them and I hurried home the long way."

"Are you real sure that's what he said?" Mrs. Benifield asked calmly. "You couldn't be mistaken, could you?"

"I heard it very clearly, I'm gonna kill you."

"You went to the sheriff and he didn't believe you, is that correct?"

"Yes, he even threatened to lock us up if we told anybody else. He said Mr. Flannery was a model citizen and we better stop telling lies about him."

"What made you think I would believe you any more than the sheriff?" she asked, looking at me and then at Imogene.

"You have to believe us," Imogen cried. "If you do, you can tell your husband and then he can make the sheriff do something."

"I'm not sure Albert can make the sheriff do anything. But I can." She stood and said, "Let me get my wrap and let's go talk to our sheriff."

She disappeared into the other room and came back with her purse and shawl which she wrapped around her shoulders. She then motioned for us to follow as she opened the door and stepped outside.

"Close the door behind you," she ordered and continued on out to the street.

Imogene and I had to hurry to keep up with her.

The sheriff wasn't in the jail when we arrived.

"I think I know where he is, come on," we left the sheriff's office and started walking south on Main Street. Stopping in front of Mildred's Eatery, she peered in the window.

"There he is stuffing his face." She opened the door and stepped inside indicating we should wait.

We watched as she approached the sheriff's table. He looked up, saw her and jumped to attention, just like a private in the Calvary, knocking over his cup of coffee.

Mrs. Benifield said something, turned and headed back out the door. The sheriff stood for a moment, picked up his napkin, wiped at the spilled coffee, put on his hat and followed behind her.

When he saw Imogene and myself, his look could have killed if it had been a weapon.

"Let's all go to the sheriff's office, shall we?" Mrs. Benifield started toward the jail.

CHAPTER EIGHT

Inside the jail, she indicated the sheriff sit at his desk. He started to say something and Mrs. Benifield shushed him, just like a child.

"Clarence," she began. "It has come to my attention that a crime has been committed and you aren't interested in pursuing the matter. Is that correct?"

"You've been listening to the tale these kids are telling. They're just a couple of trouble makers. You know as well as I do, that Flannery is an upright citizen of this town."

"That may be true, but an investigation should be done to see if there is any merit to these accusations," she said emphatically.

"But . . ."

"Don't dawdle, Clarence, come on, we'll go talk to Henry right now." She turned and headed out the door.

"You two are in a lot of trouble," he said between clenched teeth as he passed us following Mrs. Benifield out the door.

"Howdy, Mrs. Benifield. Sheriff," Flannery said as we entered the store. "What can I do for you?"

"Go ahead, Sheriff," Mrs. Benifield said, with a stern look.

"Henry," Blasingame began. "It seems that someone," he looked at Imogene and me, "somebody had accused you of something. Now, mind you, I ain't accusing you of nothing, but as the sheriff I've got to do this."

"What is it I've been accused of?" Flannery asked, surprised.

"You killed Mr. Ferguson," Imogene yelled. "I heard you tell him and I saw the body in the back room."

"You're plumb crazy," Flannery said. "Me and Bert are best friends. I wouldn't do nothing to hurt him, let alone kill him. I'm insulted that you would even consider this, Clarence."

"I know how we can clear this up very easily," said Mrs. Benifield. "Let's take a look in the back room."

"I can't let you do that," Flannery said, standing up straight. "This is private property and I refuse to give permission to search it."

"Are you just going to stand there, Sheriff?" she asked angrily.

"Henry," the sheriff said sorrowfully. "I'm afraid it don't matter if this is private property or not, we're gonna take a look in the back room."

He walked toward the door.

"I don't want you going in there," Flannery said angrily.

"I'm sorry, Henry," said Blasingame and stepped through the door.

He wasn't in the room long before he came out and said, "You want to look?" indicating the room to Mrs. Benifield and Imogene and myself.

The three of us walked through the door and stopped just inside. The room was very clean and organized.

Stacks of feed and a lot of barrels filled the room. But there was no body.

"It was right there by the back door," Imogene was crying, tears rolling down her cheeks. "It was right there," pointing to a spot by the door.

"Well, it ain't there now," exclaimed the sheriff. "I reckon you all owe Henry an apology. Henry," he turned and didn't see Flannery. "Where did he go?"

I, in the meantime was looking around the room. "Sheriff, I've got an idea. Look in those barrels. It would be the perfect place to hide a body."

"You look; I've seen all I need to see. Ain't no dead body here and that should settle it." He turned and started out of the room.

"Clarence," Mrs. Benifield's voice stopped him. "I believe you should find Henry and finish this investigation. I don't think he left because he was innocent, do you?"

He didn't answer as he continued out the front door, shaking his head.

The first four barrels were filled with grain, but the last barrel had a loose lid. I pulled it open and inside was the body of Bert Ferguson.

"Thank goodness," cried Imogene. "I'm not losing my mind."

"You young folks are to be commended for being such upright citizens. Most folks would have given up, but you didn't. You stuck to your story and now the killer will be brought to justice. That is, if the sheriff can apprehend him."

Sheriff Blasingame did indeed apprehend Mr. Flannery, arrested him and put him in jail.

As soon as word got around about what had happened, and that Imogene and I were responsible for getting the sheriff to arrest the killer, the town council decided to have a special day of celebration.

It was a festive occasion that lasted until dusk and something that I didn't much care for, but Imogene was enjoying it immensely, so I didn't say anything.

After things settled down, she looked at me with those slate blue eyes of hers and I would have done anything she wanted.

"Do you still want to sit on the swing and talk to me?" she asked.

"I sure do," I stammered. "I've got something important to ask you."

"Yes," she said.

"Yes, what'd you mean yes?"

"You're gonna ask me to marry you and the answer is yes."

"You really mean it?" I asked surprised. "You'll marry me and move to the ranch with me?"

"Of course, silly, where else would we live?"

"I need to go back to the ranch and prepare Wyatt for the surprise. Can we plan on getting married next Saturday?"

"Saturday will be fine. That'll give me time to makeover one of my dresses. I guess I should tell my parents too."

"Okay, I'm going home now and get everything ready. See you Saturday." I pecked her quickly on the lips, turned and headed to where Red was still sitting on the sidewalk.

CHAPTER NINE

"You been sitting here all this time?" I asked.

"You told me to wait, so I waited," he exclaimed.

"Well, come on, let's go home, that is if you still want to go with me."

He stood, towering over me, glanced at the mountains to the East, shook his head and said real low, "Them mountains don't feel so good no more. I go home with you."

"Let's go git the wagon. You got any more things other than what you got there?"

"Left it all back in the cabin. Didn't know if I'd need it or not."

"That's okay, we'll fix you up at home."

Mr. Garret had the team hooked up when we got to the livery stable. "I seed ye comin' and figgered you's ready to go. Gonna take him with you?" he nodded his head toward Red."

"His name is Red Walker and yes, I plan on taking him home with me."

"I's just thinking out loud. You drive safe. See you when you come back to town."

It was a quiet trip to the ranch, neither one of us said much. We pulled into the yard just before dark.

"Can't see much tonight, so I'll show you around tomorrow. Come on in and let's see if we can scare up some grub. You hungry?"

"I could eat a little something."

He had to duck as we went through the door. Wyatt was standing at the stove, stirring something in a big pot. It sure smelled good.

Red stood just inside the door, holding his rifle.

"Put your gun down and sit," I told him as I pulled out a chair.

Wyatt turned from the stove and looked at Red, then he turned those cold, calculating eyes on me as if to ask, who is this feller?

"Wyatt, this is Red. Red Walker and he's gonna be staying with us for a spell."

"You know we can't afford no extra hands right now." He turned back to the stove.

"Red ain't a hand. He's a guest. We don't have to pay a guest."

"Where's our guest gonna sleep?" he asked, sounding a little hateful.

"He can sleep in the bunkhouse; Lord knows there's plenty of room. What'cha got cooking in that pot? We're kinda hungry."

"It's chicken and dumplings if you must know and there ain't very much of it," looking over his shoulder at Red sitting there at the table.

"How about dishing up a couple of plates and let us try it out?"

He dished out two big helpings onto two plates and sort of slammed them down on the table, then turned back and put the pot back on the side of the stove to keep it warm.

"Is he mad at me?" Red asked, nodding toward Wyatt.

"Naw. He's always grumpy," I told him. "Dig in. You do like chicken and dumplings, don't you?"

"I like chicken. I don't know what dumplings is."

"I'm sure you'll like it." I told him as I shoved a spoonful into my mouth.

He looked at me with a questioning look, but lifted a spoonful to his lips, hesitated, smelled, then opened his mouth and closed his lips on it.

"Umm." He muttered around a mouthful, swallowed, then said, "This is really good."

He swiped a piece of bread in the plate sopping up the juices, shoved it in his mouth, belched rather loudly and proclaimed, "That's was one of the best meals I've had in a month of Sundays. Thanks Mr. Snow."

"Name's Wyatt. Ain't no Mr. Snow here," Wyatt said, carrying the pot to the table and poured the remaining food onto Red's plate.

"Ain't you gonna eat?" Red looked inquisitively at Wyatt.

"I et a little somethin' afore ya'll got here," Wyatt answered. "You go ahead and eat it."

"Thank you kindly, Mr. . . . oh I'm sorry. Thanks Wyatt. It's was very good."

"Yo're welcome, I reckon," he said, turning back to the stove, but not before I noticed a smile on his face. *"Maybe this is gonna work out after all,"* I thought.

"If you're finished," looking at Red. "I'll show you around a bit, then we need to get started on the nightly chores."

"You bet, I'm ready," he said, wiping his mouth on his sleeve, stood and said, "Mighty fine grub."

We went outside and headed to the barn. The cow was bellowing to be milked. It was getting late in the day for her.

"She sure is making an awful sound," Red said. "You want I should milk her fer you?"

"I'd appreciate that, then I can do some of the other things."

"Ain't you got no more hands?" he inquired as he grabbed a bucket and sat on the stool, talking, calming Bossie.

"We have two men, Amos and Angus. They're out watching the cattle," I told him as I began mucking out one of the stalls, stacking it in a wheelbarrow. Ever since Pa died, it's been mighty hard to make a go of it around here, not that it was easy when he was alive."

"I'm sure sorry about your pa. Wus you purty close with him?"

"Yeah, I reckon we were as close as a son and his pa can be. I only wish I could have been a better son while he was still here. But I'm gonna be one now. I'm gonna make this place pay off even if it puts me in the grave with him."

"I believe you'll do it too," Red said, with assurance in his voice. "You want I should carry this milk inside?"

"Naw, go dump it in the hog trough, we don't drink a lotta milk around here and that hog needs to be fattened up 'cause come winter, we're gonna invite him to a few meals." I grabbed the wheelbarrow and headed out the back door as Red went out the front.

My thought went to Imogene. *"Did I really ask her to marry me? Am I ready for marriage and a family? Seems like I can't think of nothing else when I'm around her. I reckon I better get used to the idea, 'cause she ain't gonna let me out of it."*

I dumped the mixture of manure and straw on the pile behind the barn and pushed the wheelbarrow back inside.

"That's a purty big hog you got there," Red said as he came in the barn door. "Did you say you're gonna butcher him come winter?"

"Yeah, Wyatt told me we was outta bacon before I went to town. I'd sure miss having bacon with my eggs for breakfast. Which, if you want to, you can gather the eggs from the chickens."

"I didn't see no chicken pen. You got it hid someplace?"

"No. They're what we call free range chickens. They run free in the daytime, then roost and lay their eggs in the barn. Kinda like an Easter egg hunt to find them, but it can be fun. You find them in one spot today and then that old hen tries to outsmart you the next day by laying in a new spot."

"Sounds like it might be a lot of fun. I'll give it a go."

"Use the bucket you used for milking."

"Okay," he started pushing aside the hay that I had just spread in the stalls.

"Red?"

"Yeah?"

"It ain't gonna be that easy. Why don't you check in the loft first, then work your way down here?"

"Sure," he started up the ladder swinging the bucket around one arm.

I grabbed an old tin cup and started feeding the horses what little bit of grain we had left. Maybe I should have picked up some feed while I was in town. Probably won't be able to now, with Flannery's in jail. Surely somebody'll take up where he left off with supplying feed for the county."

"I found one," I heard Red holler. "And here's another one. You wus right, this is fun."

I smiled as I loaded another load, then rolled it out back and dumped it.

"I found eight eggs," Red bragged as he climbed down the ladder. "You think I got'em all?"

"You done real good, for your first time," I told him. "Now those go in the house."

"Okay, but I'm not sure Mr. Snow likes me."

"He gave you the last of the chicken and dumplings, didn't he?" I asked.

"Yeah, I reckon he did, alright. Does that mean he likes me?" Red asked.

"Let me put it this way," I said. "If he didn't like you he wouldn't have given you the last of that meal, and that's a fact."

"Okay," he said, and started to the house swinging that bucket of eggs.

"Kind of reminded me of a little boy with his lunch pail. I'm glad I met that gentle giant. What am I saying, Gentle? I helped him kill three men, yet here now, he does seem friendly and yes, gentle. I suppose everybody has a breaking point." I thought.

I finished spreading fresh hay in the stalls, wiped my face with my bandana and shoved it back in my pocket.

"Reckon I better tell Wyatt I'm getting married. How come I feel so nervous? Maybe it's because he's like a father to me. Well, fretting about it, ain't getting it done.

CHAPTER TEN

I started walking to the house when I heard hoof beats. I turned and saw the sheriff riding into the yard. He reined up and dismounted. He looked tired and was breathing hard.

"Howdy Sheriff, what brings you out this late?"

Breathing hard, he said, "Flannery escaped and the last thing he said when I locked him up was how he was gonna take care of you and your girlfriend."

"What about Imogene?" I asked, looking hard at him.

"I checked. She wasn't home. Her ma said she didn't come home from choir practice. I went by the church and it was locked up tight." he said hanging his head. "I was kinda hoping she was with you, but I see she ain't."

"What made you think. . . oh, never mind. Let me get my gun, tell Wyatt and I'll be ready to ride."

"You got a fresh horse I can borrow?" he asked. "I rode mine pretty hard getting here."

Sure, get the Roan back in the corral. He's the best we got next to mine. While you're at it, saddle the big black for me."

I hurried to the house, walked inside, grabbed my guns and strapped them around my waist.

"Ain't that our good for nothing Sheriff Blasingame out yonder?" asked Wyatt.

"Yes, that's him, "I answered. "And I'm going with him."

"What fer? asked Wyatt. "He don't care much fer you. 'Course he don't care much fer nobody."

"Imogene is missing. I've got to find her," I told him.

"Who's Imogene?" he asked.

"She's my fiancé, and I got to find her."

"How come I ain't never heard of this Imogene?" Wyatt asked with a frown.

"I ain't got time to explain now. I got to go."

"Is that the little girl you wus talking to in town," asked Red.

"Yeah, that's her," I told him. "Now I gotta get going."

Red stood up and proclaimed, "I'm going with you."

"You don't have to do that," I told him. "You don't owe me nothing."

"I kin decide who and what I owe, I'm going with you."

"Alright," I said. "But we need to go now. Sheriff's waitin'."

"Doke, Red," Wyatt said. "You both be careful and Doke, you bring this Imogene back here so's I kin meet her."

"Okay, so long." I removed my hat and wiped my forehead, then put it back on.

"Here," Wyatt handed me a sack. "In case you git hungry." He placed his hand on my shoulder, and whispered, so only I could hear. "Please come back in one piece."

"Will do," I turned and followed Red out the door.

"He coming with us?" Blasingame nodded toward Red.

"Yes, he's coming," I told him.

"I only saddled the two horses," he replied.

"It won't take but a minute for Red to saddle Dynamite."

"Dynamite?" he questioned with a raised eyebrow.

"It's the name I picked out when I was a kid. He's probably the gentlest horse on the place. In fact, I named all the horses. The Roan you're riding is Sugarfoot and my stallion is Midnight."

Red came out of the barn leading a big, speckled gelding. Dynamite was a big horse for a giant of a man.

"You got any idea which way he headed?" I asked mounting up.

"I figure he headed for the Badlands," Blasingame answered. "He used to run with a pretty bad bunch before he settled in Crockett."

"I thought the badlands was closed down ever since The Traveler came in and cleaned it out."

"There's always a few rowdys that return, however, they don't stay long," he said. "I reckon they're afraid The Traveler will come back.

"Alright, let's ride," I gave Midnight the spurs and we were off racing out of the yard. It was a couple hours ride to the badlands. It used to be just that. A bad place where Outlaws and killers would come to hide from the law. Then one day some of the leading citizens sent for a young gunfighter called the Traveler. It seems he had dedicated his life to taking care of trouble like this. It only took him one trip into the notorious badlands and those that were left standing lit out like their tails were on fire.

Now we were headed there to see if Flannery had taken Imogene there.

"If he's hurt her, he won't live to stand trial," I thought to myself.

The sun's golden rays were peeking over the horizon, casting an eerie glow on the entrance of the canyon causing it to look like a dark cave opening.

We arrived at the entrance of the canyon which hid the dilapidated cabins and clapboard shacks.

Blasingame held up his hand indicating we should stop.

"Let's leave the horses here and go on foot and remember he's desperate. He might kill the girl if we try to rush him."

"If he touches one hair on her head, he's a dead man." I said, through clinched teeth.

"Try to keep a cool head," Blasingame told me. "Otherwise, you'll be playing into his hands."

"I've got a suggestion," Red said quietly.

"I'm listening, said Blasingame.

"Well," explained Red. "This feller don't know me. I figure I kin walk right up to him without him suspecting I'm anything other than a mountain man looking for a handout. You two can work around behind him while he's looking at me."

"It just might work," Blasingame said. "You sure you want to chance it? He might shoot you as soon as he spots you."

"I'm willing to take that chance," Red told him. "Besides, I owe Doke."

"I told you, you didn't owe me anything," I fussed at him.

"And I believe I told you I would decide who and what I owed."

"Alright, if you two have decided who owes what we need to get going," Blasingame said, sounding a little irritated.

"You be careful, Red," I told him as I placed my hand on his big shoulder. "If things don't look safe, you back outta there pronto, understand?"

"Yeah, I hear you, now git outta my way. I gotta job to do."

He laid his rifle across his arms and headed down the incline into what could be a hornet's nest.

He started whistling as soon as he got close to the first shack as if he was just out for a stroll. He was almost to the shack when a shutter flew open and a rifle barrel appeared.

Red stopped in his tracks and raised one hand while resting his rifle in the other.

"Hold on there, Partner," he said. "I don't mean no harm. I'm just looking for a little bit of something to quench this hunger in my belly. You happen to have a piece of jerky maybe?" He slowly took a step closer and then another until he was about ten feet from the window.

"I'm warning you one last time," hollered Flannery. "I'm gonna put a bullet in your eye if you don't turn around.

While Red held Flannery's attention, the sheriff and I had headed out, him to the right and me to the left.

I reached the shack before Blasingame and slid as close to the wall as possible. I could hear Flannery's voice through the thin walls. There was a problem I hadn't counted on.

I was thinking about what to do when Blasingame appeared from the right side of the building.

"There's no back door," I whispered and nodded toward the building.

"I see that," he said. "Why don't you sneak around staying as close as you can to the wall. Maybe you can get close enough to grab his rifle. I'll go this way and do the same."

"Alright," I told him. "But if he spots either one of us he may hurt Imogene."

"Understood," he nodded. "If it looks too dangerous, let Red continue his talking to him."

I started walking around the corner of the shack, then as I got closer to the front, I plastered my body next to the wall. It was slow going, but I was determined to get Imogene outta there.

As I stuck my head around the corner, Red saw me, blinked and continued to talk as if nothing was out of the ordinary.

"Please, Mister," Red was sounding pitiful, like a little child, asking for a treat. "I'm mighty thirsty and hungry.

Maybe just a drink of water? That would be the neighborly thing to do, don't you think?"

I heard the report of the rifle, saw Red grab his head and slump to the ground. I rushed around the corner and grabbed the barrel of the rifle and pulled as hard as I could. Flannery was jerked halfway out the window as he continued to hold on to his weapon.

I released my grip on the rifle, grabbed his shirt and pulled him the rest of the way out the window. He fell still clutching his rifle, which I quickly placed my foot on, causing him to cry out in pain.

I glanced away for a second and saw the sheriff was kneeling over Red. I watched as he put his ear next to Red's nose, touched his chest with his hand, looked at me and shook his head.

At that moment, I could have snuffed out this killer's life without any regrets, however, right now I had to find Imogene.

"Go ahead," Blasingame walked over. "I got this scoundrel; you see if the girl's alright?"

"What about Red?" I asked, nodding toward Red's body.

Blasingame shook his head, "He's gone. Another killing to add to Flannery's debt. He'll hang for sure."

I glanced at Red's body, then went to the front door and twisted the knob. It was locked. I walked back to the window and peeked inside. It was too dark to see anything. I climbed through the window, stopped for my eyes to adjust to the darkness, then scanned the room. Imogene wasn't here.

I walked over, unlocked the door, opened it and stepped out. I went to where the sheriff had Flannery handcuffed. Flannery was sitting up as best he could with the cuffs holding his hands behind him.

"Where is she?" I knelt down in front of him.

"Where's who?" he asked. "I don't know what you're talking about."

"Where's Imogene?" I grabbed his shirt and lifted him off the ground.

"I don't know any Imogene," he fussed. "Let me down. I'm telling you I don't know what you're talking about."

"Imogene is the girl who accused you of killing your friend, Mr. Ferguson. You remember her, don't you?"

"Sure," he said. "I remember the girl, but I never knew her name."

"Did you or didn't you threaten to get even with her and Walker here?" Blasingame asked.

"Sure, I said that," he agreed. "But I was a little upset about being accused of murder."

"You saying you didn't kill Ferguson?" Blasingame asked.

"I didn't say that," he said, shaking his head, but it was an accident. I didn't mean to kill him."

"How about that man laying over there?" the sheriff nodded toward Red. "Did you mean to kill him, or was that an accident too?"

"I knew he was with you and I couldn't let you take me back," he whined. "I don't want to hang."

"Well, you're gonna hang for sure, and that's a fact," the sheriff said emphatically.

I walked over and knelt beside Red's body. I placed my hand on his chest and felt something.

"Red," I said. "Are you alright?"

He groaned and rubbed his hand across his face. "Doke, is that you?" he asked.

"It's me, buddy. Are you okay?"

"I can't see nothing and I got one great big headache. I can't see, Doke. I can't see."

"Just lie still and I'll get some water." I started to stand.

"I'll get it," said Blasingame. "You stay with him. I sure thought he was a goner."

"Doke?" Red said, reaching out his hand. "I'm scared, Doke."

I took his hand and squeezed. "I know, Pard, but don't worry about it right now. We'll get you to a doctor and he'll fix you up good as new. Just rest now."

"Here's some water and a bandana," the sheriff handed me a canteen and a blue bandanna.

"Thanks," I poured some water on the cloth and wiped the blood from Red's head and face.

"That feels good," he said. "Thanks, you're a good friend."

"And you're an even better friend," I told him. "You shouldn't have done what you did."

"I couldn't have lived with myself if I hadn't."

Sheriff Blasingame came walking up holding the reins of all the horses. "I found Flannery's horse a couple shacks down. You ready to get going?"

"Sure, we're ready, ain't we Red? I'll help you up."

I pulled and helped Red to his feet. He swayed and I thought he was going back down, but he gained control and I led him to his horse.

"Lift your foot and I'll guide it into the stir-up. Grab the saddle horn, a little to your left. That's it. Now I'll help you. He got settled in the saddle and I climbed aboard my horse. I grabbed the reins and nodded to the sheriff who held the reins to Flannery's horse. We headed back toward town, slowly.

CHAPTER ELEVEN

We arrived back in town around nine in the morning. The shopkeepers and clerks were open and doing a brisk business.

Folks stopped what they were doing and came outside to gawk at us as we rode and stopped in front of the jail.

I helped Red out of the saddle and guided him inside the jail.

"Sit here, Red," I pushed him down into the sheriff's chair. "I'm gonna go find Doc. Hunnicutt," I told them. "You wait here with the sheriff. I'll be back as soon as I can."

Blasingame was coming out from locking Flannery in a cell and said, "Go ahead, Me and Red will be fine here."

I hurried through the door and as I turned to the right, I bumped into Imogene almost knocking her down. I quickly grabbed her to keep her from falling, pulling her close to me.

"Imogene," I said, looking into her eyes. "You're okay."

"Of course I'm okay," she said, leaning away from me. "Why wouldn't I be okay?"

"Sheriff Blasingame said you were. . .," I started to explain, but stopped and said, "Never mind that right now. I've got to find the doctor."

"Why do you need a doctor?" she asked, as we stepped away from each other. "Are you hurt?"

"It's not me, it's Red," I explained as I started to walk away.

"Who is Red?" she asked. "Is he that giant of a man who you helped in town yesterday?"

"That's him. Now I gotta go find the doctor. I'll see you later."

"Hold on and I'll go with you," grabbing my arm and falling in beside me. "What's the matter with Red, was it?"

"He got shot in the head and now he can't see."

"Who shot him? Was it Mr. Flannery?"

"Yes, it was Flannery, now come on, I got to find the doctor. By the way, where were you last night?"

"That's a rather long story," she said, breathing hard and racing to keep up with my long strides. "I'll tell you after we find the doctor."

"There he is coming out of his office. Hey, Doc! Doc!" I hollered and he looked up and saw us.

"Hello Doke and Imogene, isn't it?" he tipped his hat to Imogene.

"Doc, you need to come to the sheriff's office. Somebody's been hurt." I spoke in a hurry.

"Let me get my bag," he turned, went back inside and came out carrying his satchel. He took off at a brisk pace and Imogene and I had to hurry to keep up with him.

We reached the jail and the doctor went right in with the two of us right behind him.

"Where's the patient?" he asked Sheriff Blasingame.

"He's in one of the cells," Blasingame told him. "Didn't have no other place to put him."

"You could have brought him to my office," he headed to the cell area.

We waited in the office, silently praying for my new friend.

The doctor came out wiping his hands on a white handkerchief. "I can't make any promises, but I believe if we give it time, he will regain his sight. We don't know a lot about injuries like this, but as I stated, more than likely he'll regain his sight."

"Doke! Doke! You out there?" Red hollered.

"I'm here, buddy," I answered. "I'll be there in a couple of minutes. Imogene, you want to meet my friend?" I asked her.

"Sure," she said and grabbed my hand, letting me lead her back to the cell where Red was lying in a bunk.

"Red," I began, glancing over at Flannery in the cell across the aisle. "This is Imogene. Imogene, this is my friend, Red Walker."

"Pleased to meet you, Mr. Walker," she said, stepping close to him.

"Aw, shucks," he stuttered a little. "You don't got to call me mister, I'm just plain old Red. Doke, I sure could use a drink of water."

"Sure, Red, I'll get you some. I'll be right back."

"Imogene," I heard Red say. "You and Doke are ser "

Their voices drifted off as I went in the front room to get some water.

"How's he doing?" asked Blasingame.

"Just getting him some water," I told him. "Him and Imogene are getting acquainted."

"I wanted to tell you and her how sorry I am for treating the two of you the way I did when all this started," he said, hanging his head.

"I appreciate that, but I reckon you ought to tell Imogene," I told him, picking up the bucket of water and heading back to the cell area.

"I'm gonna do just that," the sheriff said. "I surely am."

"Here you go Red, I got you a drink." Setting the bucket on the floor and filling the dipper full.

"How 'bout giving me a drink?' asked Flannery. "I'm sure thirsty.

"I'll get to you after Red has a drink," I told him. I put my hand behind Red's head and said, "let me lift you a little so's you don't spill it all over you.

"Thanks, Doke you're a real friend," he slurped the water until the dipper was empty.

"You want some more," I asked as I lay his head back down.

"Thanks, that was enough for now. You probably should give my neighbor a drink. We wouldn't want him to die of thirst."

"No, we sure wouldn't want that to happen," I filled the dipper and handed it to Flannery.

"That's real decent if you, Walker," he told me while trying to drink through the bars of the cell, spilling the majority of it. "I'm having a little bit of trouble as you can see. How about getting the sheriff to open this door long enough for me to drink this water?"

"I reckon you'll have to make do with the way things are, at least for now," taking the dipper back and placing it in the bucket.

"Imogene," I said. "I think you and I need to talk. Red, if you'll excuse us, we need to go talk."

"Sure Doke. You two go ahead. Imogene, I'm sure glad I got to meet you, although I wish I could see you."

"You'll be seeing her real soon," I told him. "If you need anything, holler for the sheriff."

I took Imogene's hand and we walked into the office.

"Miss Imogene," the sheriff began. "I'm mighty sorry about the way I treated you when you came and told me about Flannery. I hope you'll forgive me."

"I don't know if I should, Sheriff," she said hatefully. "I'm not the first person you've disrespected in this town."

"I know, ma'am, and I'm trying to turn over a new leaf and be a sheriff that everyone respects. It would sure make me feel better if you could find it in your heart to give me that chance."

"I can do that on one condition," she told him.

"What's the condition," he asked.

"I forgive you on the condition that I see an improvement in your actions."

"I reckon I can do that," he said, wiping his hand across his face. "Thank you."

I nodded to the sheriff and we went out the door.

"Let's go sit on the bench in front of the general store and you can tell me where you were last night."

"Okay," she answered.

We sat on the bench and I turned toward her with a questioning look on my face.

"Well," she began. "This is what happened. I was on my way back from choir practice when I tripped and bumped my head. I don't remember anything until my ma was shaking me asking if I was alright."

"Are you alright?" I asked concerned.

"I'm fine, but I do have a headache. The doctor said I would probably have it for a couple of days. Ma said the sheriff came by asking for me last night. Do you know why he wanted me?"

"He thought Flannery had kidnapped you when he broke outta jail. Thank goodness he didn't. You might have more than a headache if he had."

"I didn't know Flannery had broken outta jail," she said. "Is that where Red got shot? While you were bringing back Flannery?" she reached her hand and ran it through her hair.

"Are you sure you're okay?" I asked concerned.

"Like I told you, just a little headache. I told my mother about us getting married and she's very excited and happy for us. She did suggest, and that's what it is, a suggestion, but she suggested we wait until the middle of summer. I told her I would talk to you and we would decide together and let her know. What do you want to do?"

"I think you know what I want to do, but I'll do whatever you want to do. Then again, it would give me time to work on the house and get it a fit place for a female to live in. Please don't misunderstand what I'm saying. I love you and I want to marry you more than anything in the world, but perhaps I was a little hasty when I asked you to marry me. The house really needs some fixing up and of course we need to figure out where Wyatt is gonna sleep. I'm not so sure he's gonna want to sleep in the bunkhouse."

"Where has he been sleeping?"

"He's sleeps in Pa's bedroom. We ain't got but two bedrooms."

"I don't know why he can't continue to sleep there. After all, we won't be needing two bedrooms, will we?" she asked with that twinkle in her eyes.

"No," I assured her. "We sure won't need two bedrooms. But that still leaves the problem of the house not being ready for you to move in."

"Are you saying you want to wait?"

"I don't want to wait, but I do want the place to be fit for you."

"Alright then, we'll wait, but how long?"

"I reckon your Ma had the right idea. How about June first?"

"That sounds perfect. I always wanted to be a June bride."

"Then it's settled. June first. That'll give me plenty of time. And there is one more thing."

"What's that?"

"I love you Imogene Cooper. And that's a fact."

65

Epilogue:

Flannery's trial was held a month later when the circuit judge came to town. The trial lasted only three hours. The jury voted unanimously that he be hanged, but not in our town. He was transferred to the county seat by the newly elected Sheriff Blasingame, where his sentence was to be carried out one week after his trial.

Red Walker regained his sight and decided to go back to his beloved mountains where he met and married an Indian chief's daughter.

Doke and Imogene got married June first and moved into their newly renovated home. Wyatt Snow gladly moved to the bunkhouse, he said, "'cause I don't figger newlyweds need no company."

The ranch prospered and became one of the largest in the territory.

The Walkers had three girls and one boy, whom they named after Doke's pa. Frank Walker the second.

I do believe his pa would be proud.

Books by J.C. Hulsey

Angel Falls, Texas
Velvet Sky, Arizona
Angry Orchard, Colorado
Clear Stone, Wyoming
Itching Tree, Idaho
Windy Butte, New Mexico
Devil's Dance, Dakota Territory
Redemption Road
Red Rose
Rebecca
The Concho Kid
Ugly Mugly
GUTSHOT
The Last Ride
The Old Man
The Pistol Preacher
Shortland
Dynamite
The Concho Kid
Dead Man's Gun
Does Nora Know
Doke Walker
Brothers
Echo Mountain
Satan's Refuge
Shadrack
The Brute
The Decision
The Greenhorn
The Gunfight
The Hangman